Oliver and Amanda

and

Amanda Pig, First Grader

by Jean Van Leeuwen
pictures by Ann Schweninger

DIAL BOOKS FOR YOUNG READERS

For Debbie Lenaghan and her class
of '06, terrific teachers all.
−J.V.L.

For Jan
−A.S.

DIAL BOOKS FOR YOUNG READERS
A division of Penguin Young Readers Group
Published by The Penguin Group
Penguin Group (USA) Inc., 375 Hudson Street, New York, NY 10014, U.S.A.
Penguin Group (Canada), 90 Eglinton Avenue East, Suite 700, Toronto, Ontario, Canada M4P 2Y3
(a division of Pearson Penguin Canada Inc.)
Penguin Books Ltd, 80 Strand, London WC2R 0RL, England
Penguin Ireland, 25 St. Stephen's Green, Dublin 2, Ireland (a division of Penguin Books Ltd)
Penguin Group (Australia), 250 Camberwell Road, Camberwell, Victoria 3124, Australia
(a division of Pearson Australia Group Pty Ltd)
Penguin Books India Pvt Ltd, 11 Community Centre, Panchsheel Park, New Delhi - 110 017, India
Penguin Group (NZ), Cnr Airborne and Rosedale Roads, Albany, Auckland 1310, New Zealand
(a division of Pearson New Zealand Ltd)
Penguin Books (South Africa) (Pty) Ltd, 24 Sturdee Avenue, Rosebank, Johannesburg 2196, South Africa
Penguin Books Ltd, Registered Offices: 80 Strand, London WC2R 0RL, England
Text copyright © 2007 by Jean Van Leeuwen
Pictures copyright © 2007 by Ann Schweninger
Manufactured in China on acid-free paper
The Dial Easy-to-Read logo is a registered trademark of
Dial Books for Young Readers, a division of Penguin Young Readers Group
® TM 1,162,718.
3 5 7 9 10 8 6 4
Library of Congress Cataloging-in-Publication Data
Van Leeuwen, Jean.
Amanda Pig, first grader / by Jean Van Leeuwen ; pictures by Ann Schweninger.
p. cm.
Summary: Amanda is very excited about starting first grade, and although everything is not exactly as she expected,
she soon begins learning to read and finding her way.
ISBN-13: 978-0-8037-3181-3
[1. Schools—Fiction. 2. Books and reading—Fiction. 3. Pigs—Fiction.] I. Schweninger, Ann, ill. II. Title.
PZ7.V3273Anr 2007
[E]—dc22
2006010409
Reading Level 1.9

The full-color artwork was prepared using carbon pencil, colored pencils, and watercolor washes.

CONTENTS

The First Day

"Good-bye, First Grader!" called Mother.

"Have fun!" said Father.

Amanda climbed the bus steps.

They didn't seem as high as last year.

"Hi, Amanda! Sit with me!"

said her best friend, Lollipop.

Amanda was so excited, she bounced.

"I can't wait for first grade!" she said.

"We don't have to take naps

   and we get to play on the big playground

   and have real desks and jobs

   and homework.

   And we'll know how to read!"

But Lollipop wasn't bouncing.

"What if we can't find our room?"

she said. "And our teacher isn't nice?

And the big kids on the big playground

are mean to us?"

"Don't worry," said Amanda.

"First grade is going to be great!"

When they got off the bus, Amanda said,

"Oliver, will you take us to Room 6?"

But Oliver and his friends were gone.

"Never mind," said Amanda.

"We'll find it ourselves."

They walked past the kindergarten.

"Look how little they are!" she said.

They walked past the art room

and the music room.

"We'll never find Room 6," said Lollipop.

"We'll be late and our teacher will be mad."

They turned a corner.

And there it was, Room 6.

"We did it!" said Amanda.

"Good morning, First Graders,"

said the teacher.

"My name is Mrs. Mary Ann Pig

and I can't wait to get to know you!"

"I knew she would be nice," said Amanda.

She sat down at her real desk.

She lined up her new pencils on top.

"I love it!" she said.

Mrs. Mary Ann Pig gave them jobs.

"I get to lead the pledge to the flag!"

said Amanda.

She said the pledge very loud.

Then the first graders got to work.

They drew pictures, and counted pennies.

After that, it was time for recess.

"Come on, Lollipop!" said Amanda.

They went on the big slide

and big swings and big climbing bars.

"That was fun," said Lollipop.

"And no one was even mean to us."

After lunch, it was reading time.

Mrs. Mary Ann Pig let each of them

choose a book.

Amanda picked one about a princess.

"Finally," she thought, "I can read!"

She looked at the first page.

What was wrong?

She knew her letters. "O, N, C, E."

But she didn't know the words.

She couldn't read.

Amanda looked at the pictures

and made up her own story.

Soon it was time to go home.

Lollipop passed out papers.

"Wow!" said Amanda. "Homework!"

Then she climbed on the bus.

"How was first grade?" asked Mother.

"Mostly great," said Amanda.

"But partly bad.

My teacher is nice. But I can't read.

I thought I could read in first grade."

"Don't worry," said Mother. "You will."

Lost and Found

Mrs. Mary Ann Pig wrote words

on the blackboard.

"This is our word wall," she said.

"We will be learning these words

and adding new ones."

Sam already knew all the words.

Lollipop knew seven.

Amanda only knew two. "I" and "and."

She still couldn't read.

She felt sad.

But then Mrs. Mary Ann Pig said,

"I need someone for an important job.

Amanda, will you do it?"

Amanda smiled. She loved jobs.

"Please take this note to the office,"

said Mrs. Mary Ann Pig.

Amanda held the note tight.

She walked to the end of the hall.

"The office is this way," she said.

"Or is it that way?"

She turned right.

Amanda looked in a door.

All she saw were books.

18

"That's not the office," she said.

"It's the library."

She kept walking.

Amanda looked in another door.

All she saw were kids at long tables

and chairs.

And all she smelled was lunch.

"That's not the office," she said.

"It's the lunch room."

She came to the end of the hall.

"This way or that way?" she said.

"Which way is the right way?

Hey, that's a poem!"

She turned left.

Amanda peeked in another door.

All she saw were kids running
and jumping rope and playing ball.
And all she heard was noise.
"That's not the office," she said.
"It's the gym. But how did it get here?
I'm all mixed up!"

Amanda was tired from walking.
She was hungry from smelling lunch.
"Maybe I should go back to my room,"
she said.

But she didn't know how to get back.

"Maybe I could find Oliver

and he would take me back," she said.

But Oliver's room was upstairs.

Amanda had never been upstairs.

She sat down next to a big box.

A tear plopped onto the note.

"Are you lost?" asked someone.

It was the principal, Mr. James Pig.

"Yes," sniffed Amanda.

"You came to the right place,"
    said Mr. James Pig. "Do you know
    what it says on this box?"

"What?" said Amanda.

"'Lost and Found,'" said Mr. James Pig.

"I was trying to find the office,"
    said Amanda. "But I got lost."

"You did find it," said Mr. James Pig.

"Look."

Right next to the box was the office door.

Amanda smiled.

She gave Mr. James Pig the note.

"Thanks," he said.

"Thanks for finding me," said Amanda.

And Mr. James Pig walked Amanda

all the way back to her room.

The Big Kids

"I know two new words," said Amanda.

"'Lost' and 'found.'"

"Very good," said Mrs. Mary Ann Pig.

She wrote them on the word wall.

At recess, Lily said, "Let's play kickball."

"We can't play here," said Sam.

"See that sign? 'No Ball Playing.'"

"Hooray!" said Amanda.

"Now I know three more words."

They played kickball in the grass.

Lily kicked a good one.

It went over William's head, down the hill,

onto the field where the big kids played.

"Uh-oh!" said Lollipop.

"Give us back our ball!" cried Sam.

"It's our ball now," said a big kid.

"It is *not*!" said Lily. "It's ours."

"Too bad," said the big kid.

He ran away with the first-grade ball.

"I told you the big kids
    would be mean to us," said Lollipop.

"What should we do?" said William.

"We could tell our teacher," said Lily.

"We can get it back ourselves,"
    said Amanda. "We'll just ask nicely."

"You can ask nicely," said William.

"I'll stay here."

Slowly she walked down the hill.

What would she say to the big kids?

What if they were really mean?

All of a sudden, her knees felt funny.

"Wait!" said Lollipop. "I'm coming too."

"Me too," said Lily and Sam and William.

"But you can do the talking,"
   said William.

Three boys were playing with the ball.

A big kid and a bigger big kid

and the biggest big kid.

The biggest big kid had the ball.

Amanda had to look way up

like she was talking to a tree.

"Please," she said, "give us our ball."

"Why should we?" said the biggest big kid.

"Because it's the first-grade ball,"

said Amanda. "And we need it

and you have your own ball,

so it's not fair to take ours."

The biggest big kid looked down at her.

"So?" he said.

"Well, you know what else?" said Amanda.

"I have a big brother and he's really big!"

"What grade is he in?"

 asked the bigger big kid.

"Um—" said Amanda. "Second."

"Is his name Oliver?" asked the big kid.

"Yes," said Amanda.

"Oliver is my friend," he said.

"If you're his sister, you must be okay.

Give her the ball, Henry."

The biggest big kid gave Amanda the ball.

"Thanks," said Amanda.

She and her friends walked up the hill.

"That wasn't *so* bad," said William.

"They weren't *so* mean," said Lollipop.

"No," said Amanda. "I just asked nicely."

Reading Time

Amanda saw signs everywhere.

"Push," said the sign on the gym door.

"No Parking," said the sign

in front of the school.

"Stop," said the sign out the bus window.

She knew more and more words.

"Pretty soon I'll be able to read,"

said Amanda. "Maybe."

One day it was Lollipop's birthday.

She brought cupcakes to school.

And Mrs. Mary Ann Pig wrote

two new words on the word wall.

"Cake!" said Lollipop.

"Balloon!" said Amanda. "It's like 'ball,'

but bigger."

After lunch, everyone had cupcakes.

"My mom made lots," said Lollipop.

"Can I take them to other classes?"

"Yes," said Mrs. Mary Ann Pig.

"And Amanda can go with you."

They went to the kindergarten.

After that, not many cupcakes were left.

They went to the library.

"Happy birthday!" said the librarian.

They went to the nurse's office.

"Delicious!" said the nurse.

One cupcake was left.

"Let's take it to the office," said Amanda.

"I don't know the way," said Lollipop.

"I do," said Amanda.

She turned left and right and left again.

And there was the office.

"Thank you!" said Mr. James Pig.

"Shall I walk you back to your room?"

"No, thank you," said Amanda.

"We can find it ourselves."

When they got back, it was reading time.

Amanda picked the princess book again.

"'Once,'" she said. "'Once up—'

'Once upon a time.' Hey, I'm reading!"

"How exciting!" said Mrs. Mary Ann Pig.

"I'm going to read this whole book,"
said Amanda.

She didn't know all the words. Not yet.

But she was reading!

"Time for recess," said Mrs. Mary Ann Pig.

Everyone put on their jackets.

Everyone except Amanda.

"Come on, Amanda," said Lollipop.

"Just a minute," said Amanda.

Everyone lined up at the door.

Everyone except Amanda.

"Hey, Amanda!" said Sam.

"Don't you want to play kickball?"

"I do," said Amanda.

"But I can't help it. I can't stop reading!"

"You may stay inside today,"

said Mrs. Mary Ann Pig.

Then everyone went out to recess.

Everyone except Amanda.

She kept reading and reading

and reading.

And she finished the whole book.